WRITTEN BY JON SCIESZKA

CHARACTERS AND ENVIRONMENTS DEVELOPED BY THE

DAVID SHANNON   LOREN LONG   DAVID GORDON

ILLUSTRATION CREW:

Executive producer: TOT INDUSTRIES in association with Animagic S.L.

Creative supervisor: Sergio Pablos ○ Drawings by: Juan Pablo Navas ○ Color by: Isabel Nadal

Color assistant: Gabriela Lazbal ○ Art director: Karin Paprocki

Ready-to-Read

Simon Spotlight

New York   London   Toronto   Sydney   New Delhi

SIMON SPOTLIGHT

An imprint of Simon & Schuster Children's Publishing Division

1230 Avenue of the Americas, New York, New York 10020

Text and illustrations copyright © 2009 by JRS Worldwide, LLC.

SIMON SPOTLIGHT, READY-TO-READ and colophon are registered trademarks of Simon & Schuster, Inc.

TRUCKTOWN and JON SCIESZKA'S TRUCKTOWN and design are trademarks of JRS Worldwide, LLC.

For information about special discounts for bulk purchases, please contact

Simon & Schuster Special Sales at 1-866-506-1949 or business@simonandschuster.com.

The Simon & Schuster Speakers Bureau can bring authors to your live event.

For more information or to book an event contact the Simon & Schuster Speakers Bureau at

1-866-248-3049 or visit our website at www.simonspeakers.com.

The text of this book was set in Truck King. / Manufactured in the United States of America

1213 LAK / First Simon Spotlight edition / 10 9 8 7 6 5 4 3 2 1

Library of Congress Cataloging-in-Publication Data / Scieszka, Jon.

Uh-oh Max / written by Jon Scieszka ; characters and environments developed by

the Design Garage: David Shannon, Loren Long, David Gordon.

p. cm—(Jon Scieszka's Trucktown. Ready-to-roll.)

Summary: When Max gets in trouble after speeding up a ramp, all of his Trucktown friends try

to help out.

[1. Traffic accidents—Fiction. 2. Trucks—Fiction.] I. Design Garage. II. Title.

PZ7.S41267Uh 2009   [E]—dc22   2007027809

ISBN 978-1-4814-1461-6 (hc)

ISBN 978-1-4169-4141-5 (pbk)

Max **jumps.**

Max flies.

"TO THE MAX!"

he cheers.

Uh-oh.

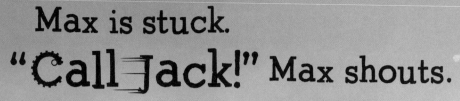

Max is stuck.
"Call Jack!" Max shouts.

Jack pushes.

No luck. Max is stuck.

"Call Kat!"

Max shouts.

Kat digs.

No luck. Max is stuck.

"Call Gabby!"

Max shouts.

Gabby talks . . .

and talks . . .

and talks.

Really no luck.
Max is **really** stuck.
Who can help?

"Do you want an ice cream?
Do you want an ice cream?
Do you want an ice cream?"

An ice cream won't help.

The Fire Truck twins?

Tow Truck Ted?
Of course!

Ted **hooks** Max.
Ted **flips** Max.

"Hurray for Ted!"

Max zooms.

Max jumps.

HERE WE
GO AGAIN!

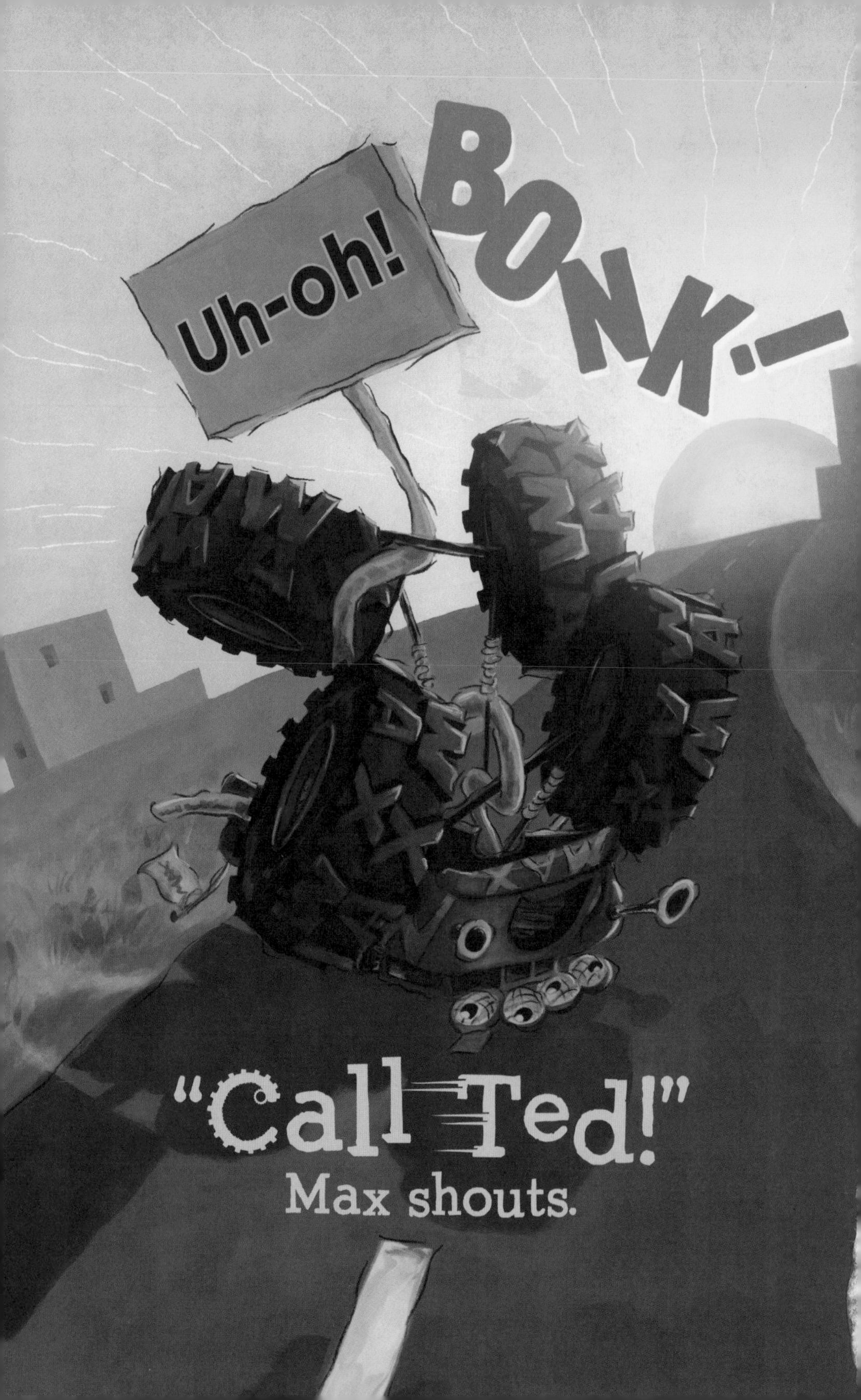

"Call Ted!"
Max shouts.